Fairy Charm

ROS

ORCHARD

This is the Secret Kingdom

The Golden Palace

Contents

A Message from King Merry

Ellie Macdonald smiled as she put the finishing touches to her sketch of a pyramid. She and her best friends, Summer Hammond and Jasmine Smith, were in their classroom at Honeyvale School making a poster about Ancient Egypt as a class project. Next to Ellie, Jasmine was humming under her breath

as she wrote out a list of different
Egyptian gods, and on the other side of
Ellie, Summer was playing with the end
of one of her blonde plaits as she looked
through a book. Around them, the rest
of the class were working hard on their
posters too.

"What do you think?" Ellie asked,
showing Summer and Jasmine her picture.

"It's great," said Summer.

"It really is," Jasmine agreed. "Maybe
you should draw a mummy next?"

"Sure." Ellie's green eyes sparkled. "Hey,
what are a mummy's favourite flowers?"

"I don't know," said Summer.

Ellie grinned. "Chrysanthe*mummies* of
course!"

Jasmine and Summer groaned.

"That's awful, Ellie!" Jasmine said.

"I can think of some more jokes if you like," said Ellie.

"No, save us." Jasmine pretended to plead.

Summer giggled. "We'd better get on with this poster, you two," she said. "I think I might write something about the pyramids now. Did you know the Ancient Egyptians used to put traps inside them?"

"Why?" asked Ellie, intrigued.

"To stop thieves who tried to steal the treasure," said Summer.

"What sort of traps?" Jasmine asked.

"Well, sometimes they'd build a complicated maze so the thieves would get lost, or they might leave snakes in the tunnels, or build a concealed pit for the thieves to fall into."

"Oh, wow!" said Jasmine. "I'd love to

explore a pyramid. It would be a real adventure."

Summer shivered. "I'm not sure about the sound of all those traps…"

"Well, how about an adventure somewhere a bit more magical?" Ellie whispered with a smile.

Summer grinned back. "Definitely! Every adventure in the Secret Kingdom is fun."

The three friends exchanged happy looks. The Secret Kingdom was an enchanted land filled with magical creatures, and they were the only humans who knew about it! They owned a wonderful magic box that had been made by King Merry, the jolly ruler of the kingdom. Whenever King Merry needed the girls' help he would send them a message using the box.

"Going to the Secret Kingdom is the most fun *ever*," said Jasmine.

Ellie nodded enthusiastically. "Even if we do usually have to deal with Queen Malice and her horrible Storm Sprites," she added.

Queen Malice was King Merry's wicked sister. She kept hatching plots to try and take over the kingdom. So far, Summer, Ellie and Jasmine had always managed to stop her.

"Oh, I wish we could go to the Secret Kingdom again," Jasmine said, longingly.

Ellie nodded. "I checked the Magic Box ten times yesterday, but there was no message."

Just then, their teacher clapped her hands. "Time to pack away everyone!" she called.

The girls began to clear up. While Jasmine and Summer were putting away their textbooks, Ellie nipped into the cloakroom. Her school bag was hanging under her coat, and the Magic Box was inside it. She checked over her shoulder to make sure no one was watching and then undid the buckles. Would the Magic Box be shining at last, like it always did when King Merry sent them a message…?

But no. The carved wooden box wasn't glowing at all.

"No luck," she said, returning to the others. "There's no message yet."

Jasmine sighed. She really wished they could whizz off to the Secret Kingdom. They always had so much fun

– whether they were having exciting adventures fighting Queen Malice, making new friends, or joining in with magical celebrations. It was the best place ever!

At breaktime, Summer, Ellie and Jasmine joined in a game of hopscotch with a few of their other friends in the playground. They took their bags with them and left them in a pile. Ellie was waiting for her turn at hopscotch when she glanced over and saw her bag was glowing faintly. She gasped.

Olivia, who was in front of her in the line, glanced at her. "What's the matter?"

"N–nothing," Ellie said quickly. "Gosh, look how fast Sasha's doing the hopscotch."

Olivia turned back to watch their

other friend. Ellie turned quickly towards Jasmine and Summer, who were standing behind her. Using her eyes, she caught their attention and nodded meaningfully towards her bag. They saw the glow too. Summer's hand flew to her mouth.

"You know, I think I'll give hopscotch a miss this breaktime," Jasmine said loudly.

"Me too," said Ellie and Summer.

"OK, see you later," called Olivia and Sasha as Ellie, Summer and Jasmine ran over to the pile of bags. Ellie scooped her bag up and hugged it to her chest, covering it with her arms so that no one in the playground could see it was glowing.

"There must be a message from King

Merry," said Summer.

"Let's find somewhere private to have a look," Jasmine said quickly.

Ellie's eyes shone. "I have a feeling we're about to go to the Secret Kingdom again!"

A Mystery to Solve

The three friends ran behind the Reception classroom, where the playground was quiet. Ellie looked around cautiously and then took the Magic Box out of her bag. It was glowing softly.

"That's a bit odd. It's not shining as brightly as usual, is it?" Ellie said. "Normally it really sparkles and gleams."

Jasmine pointed to the words that were scrolling across the mirrored lid. "There is a message, though!"

Summer read the words out:

"Seek a glittering forest, find
a building of gold
Say its name quickly, be brave
and be bold."

She looked at the others. "The riddle definitely *sounds* like the usual sort of message King Merry sends. Quick, let's solve it, and then when Trixi gets here we can ask her why the box isn't glowing as brightly as usual."

"Good plan," said Jasmine.

Trixi was King Merry's royal pixie. She always arrived to whisk them away to

the Secret Kingdom as soon as they had
worked out the correct answer to the
riddle.

"Hang on," said Ellie, frowning
suddenly. "The map hasn't come out of
the box like it usually does, either."

Normally when they read the riddle
out loud, the box opened and a special
map floated out. Summer tapped the lid
of the box experimentally. The lid slowly
opened with a creak. The magic map of
the Secret Kingdom remained folded up
in one of the compartments inside.

"That's weird," said Jasmine, taking the
map out. She unfolded it. "OK, the riddle
says we need to find a glittering forest.
Can anyone see one?"

They all peered at the map. The
pictures on it usually moved, but today

everything seemed to be in slow motion – the pixies skiing down the Frosty Slopes, the dream dragons flying through Dream Valley, the water nymphs playing around Clearsplash Waterfall.

"Here!" said Ellie suddenly, pointing at a deep forest of green, bronze and golden-leaved trees hidden far away in one corner of the Secret Kingdom. "What about this forest?" Hidden amongst the trees swaying slowly on the magical map was an elegant palace made of gold, with thin tall spires.

Jasmine read the label out: "*The Golden Palace.* That *must* be the answer to the riddle. It's a building of gold in a glittering forest. Let's try saying the name!"

The girls put their hands on to the

Magic Box. "The Golden Palace!" they announced in unison.

Suddenly a small, green ball of light came shooting out of the box. The light zigged and zagged randomly around their heads.

"Whoa!" they heard a tinkly little voice cry out. "Stop, leaf, stop!"

The ball of light hovered in front of the girls' noses and then with a faint, silvery *pop* it turned into a green leaf. Kneeling on the leaf was Trixibelle, the royal pixie. She was wearing a beautiful pink knee-length beaded dress that glimmered and sparkled, but her blonde curls were very tousled.

"Goodness me, that was a bumpy ride!" she gasped, jumping to her feet. "I don't know what's the matter with my leaf today. Hello, girls!"

"Hi, Trixi," said Ellie, delighted to see their friend. "What's happening in the Secret Kingdom? Is something going on?"

"The Magic Box and the map don't seem to be working quite like they usually do," Summer added.

"Oh dear," said Trixi. "Not those as well. Something definitely isn't right in the Secret Kingdom. No one's magic seems to be working as it usually does. King Merry is very worried that it's going to affect the Golden Ball."

"The Golden Ball?" asked Jasmine. "What's that?"

"It's a celebration that Prince Felix, the prince of the Golden Forest Fairies, holds each year at his Golden Palace," Trixi explained. "King Merry is already at the

Golden Palace, and he really wants you
to meet him there. That's if you'd like to,
of course?"

"Like to? We'd love to!" said Jasmine.

Summer and Ellie nodded quickly in
agreement.

Trixi beamed. "I hoped you'd say that!"

The girls held hands. Trixi tapped her
ring and called out:

"To the most glittering palace ever seen,
Take us swiftly by limousine!"

Nothing happened.

The girls exchanged anxious looks.
Why hadn't Trixi's magic whisked them
away?

"Come on, ring, please work!" Trixi
begged.

She tapped the ring hard, and this time a burst of green sparkles sputtered out. They surrounded the girls, spinning slowly at first but getting faster and faster until they finally felt themselves being lifted into the air and swept away.

Round and round, Summer, Ellie and Jasmine spun in the cloud of sparkles, until they landed with a slight bump on their bottoms.

Ellie opened her eyes. "Look!"

They were sitting in an old-fashioned limousine – but it was made completely of gold! It was speeding along an avenue of gold and bronze trees.

"There's no driver!" Summer exclaimed, pointing at the empty front seat. The steering wheel was moving all by itself as they drove around a corner. "Oh, wow!"

"This limousine works by magic," said Trixi. "It doesn't need a driver." She was perched on her leaf on the dashboard in front of them.

"This is amazing!" said Jasmine, settling back against the soft cushions and feeling

like a movie star. They were no longer
wearing their school uniforms. Trixi's
magic had changed their clothes into
beautiful beaded party dresses. Jasmine's
was bright a soft grey, Ellie's was a
purple that brought out the deep green of
her eyes and Summer's was a lovely pale
pink. They all wore matching sparkly
ballet pumps on their feet and delicate
tiaras were nestling in their hair. The
tiaras always appeared when the girls
arrived in the Secret Kingdom – they
showed everyone that the girls were Very
Important Friends of King Merry.

"I love my dress," said Ellie.

"Me too," said Summer, stroking the
pretty beads.

"You need special clothes if you're
going to come to the Golden Ball,"

Trixi told them.

"Is that the Golden Palace?" asked Jasmine, pointing ahead to where a beautiful golden building was glowing through the trees.

"Yes. We'll be there any minute," said Trixi.

But just as she spoke, the car swerved, and Trixi was catapulted off the dashboard!

Magical Mishaps

Summer flung herself forward and caught the little pixie just as she was about to hit the floor at their feet. Jasmine grabbed the wheel and righted it and the car set off again towards the palace.

"What happened?" gasped Ellie.

"I think it was the limousine's magic going wrong," said Trixi. "Something still seems to be affecting all the magic in the kingdom."

"Do you think it's to do with Queen Malice?" said Summer. "Whenever things go wrong, she's usually to blame."

"It might be." Trixi's forehead wrinkled in a tiny frown. "Oh, I do hope she's not been thinking up another horrible plot."

"If Queen Malice is up to something we'll stop her, Trixi, don't worry," declared Jasmine.

Ellie nodded vigorously. "Let's get to the palace and work out what's going on!"

To the girls' relief, nothing more went wrong with the limousine and it came to a stop safely beside the grand front door. The palace had a round circular driveway in front of it, with a fountain in the centre made from a golden tree. Water tinkled from the end of each branch into a sparkling pool that was

lined with a mosaic of small gold tiles.
The girls stared at it, amazed.

"Hang on a minute," Jasmine said

suddenly. "If the prince is a fairy prince,
why isn't his palace really small? The
fairies we met when we went to Glitter
Beach were all about your size, Trixi."

"Ah, but you see, Prince Felix is a

Golden Forest fairy," said Trixi. "They're tall with beautiful, glittering, golden skin."

Two gnome guards were standing either side of the huge front door. They were dressed in gold and purple uniforms with long pikestaffs. They looked quite fierce with hooked noses and big broad shoulders, but as they saw the girls and Trixi getting out of the car, friendly smiles spread across their wrinkled faces.

"Welcome, friends!" they said, hurrying forward.

"This is Albus and Tobias," Trixi told the girls. "They're Prince Felix's guards."

"You must be Jasmine, Summer and Ellie," said Albus, looking at their tiaras and bowing low. "It's an honour to meet you."

Tobias bowed too. "Prince Felix will be very glad you've made it here for the ball."

"How are the preparations going?" Trixi asked anxiously.

"Not very well," said Tobias. "None of the party magic seems to be working properly and the prince doesn't know what to do."

"We'll try to help," said Summer.

"Oh, I hope you can," said Albus.

Tobias opened the door and beckoned the girls and Trixi through. They walked into an amazing hallway with a domed golden ceiling and beautiful murals on the wall – each showing a forest scene.

"It's incredible!" breathed Ellie, looking round. There was a painting of a new-born fawn lying beside its mother in a clearing, another of a family of foxes playing, and a third picture of trees shedding their leaves in autumn while bluebirds swooped

through the branches.

"Greetings, Trixibelle!" A tall young man came striding across the hall towards them. He had jet-black hair, pointed ears, eyes the colour of new green moss and skin that shimmered as if it was coated with golden dust. Large shimmering wings were folded close against his back.

"Prince Felix!" Trixi said, smoothing her curls.

"It's lovely to see you!" She flew on her leaf around his head. "These are our Very Important Friends – Jasmine, Summer and Ellie."

"Enchanted to meet you, girls," said the prince, sweeping into a low bow. He was wearing a red and green tunic over green leggings and pointy golden boots. "King Merry is here somewhere. He's—"

"Crowns and sceptres! It's my dear friends at last! Oh, I'm so glad you could come!" King Merry came hurrying out of the ballroom towards them. He was wearing a top hat with his crown perched at an angle on top, shiny black shoes and a smart purple jacket with golden piping that was long at the back and only just met over his very round tummy. His half-moon spectacles were slipping down his nose as usual, but his eyes were twinkling brightly in his kind face.

The girls ran forward and hugged him. "It's lovely to see you, King Merry," said Summer.

"Are you ready to dance and have

fun?" King Merry asked. "I've been practising my moves for the ball." He spun round in a circle holding his arms as if he had an imaginary partner in them. "I can't wait to try out my steps on Prince Felix's floating dance floor."

Prince Felix cleared his throat. "Ah yes, well, um, that's if the floating dance floor can be persuaded to float. Look!" He led the way into the ballroom. It had big glass chandeliers hanging from the ceiling and windows carved in the shape of wings. At one end of the ballroom there was a rainbow-coloured stage that was floating a few centimetres above the normal floor.

"Oh dear," said Trixi.

"What?" said Jasmine.

"The dance floor is supposed to be

floating high in the air," Prince Felix
explained. "There's usually a slide down
from it that leads to a sea of cushions
but that's vanished and the floor will
only float a few centimetres. And that's
not all. The No Hand Band seem to
have forgotten how to play music." He
gestured into one corner where various

musical instruments
were
playing
themselves
– flutes were
floating in the
air, violins had
bows hovering
over them and
piano keys
were
moving up
and down
as if pressed
by invisible
fingers. The sounds that were coming out
were just strangled high-pitched notes.

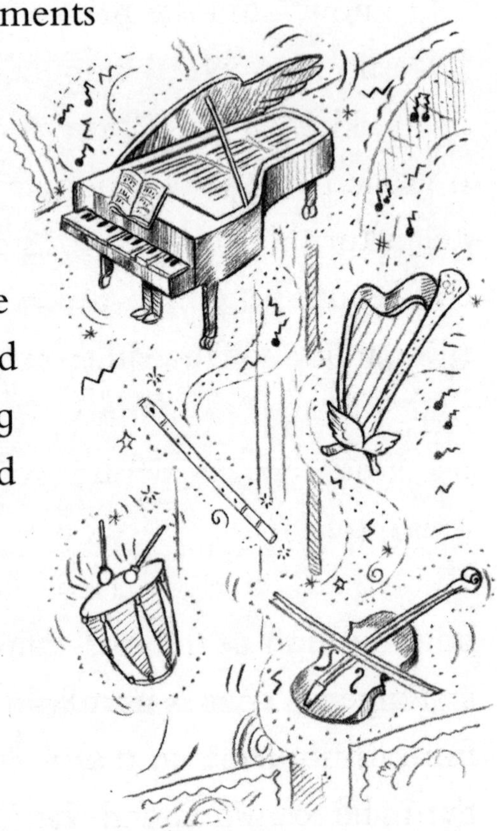

"No one could dance to that," said
Jasmine.

"I know," said the prince glumly. "I have no idea what's happening. The chefs in the kitchen are all running round in a panic because the magical finger food keeps turning to pieces of stale bread, and the beautiful twinkle-tinkle bunting in the garden has turned to scraps of grey paper. My party planners are trying to fix things, but they can't work out what's going on."

Just then, an elf hurried past the window outside. He was dressed in a sparkly suit with a party hat perched on top of his purple hair, and as he noticed them, he leaned in through one of the open windows. "I'm terribly sorry, Prince Felix, but it seems we can't even get the flowers to grow in the garden! There are supposed to be pink and white roses everywhere but every time we use some of our Grow-Faster Powder, the roses just shrivel up. Look!"

Everyone went over to the window and looked outside. There were flowerpots placed all round the gardens with rose bushes planted in them. The elf drew a tiny pouch out of his pocket and took a pinch of silver powder from inside it. He sprinkled it over a nearby pot. The roses in it instantly shrivelled up.

"That's awful!" said Prince Felix.

"I know! This Grow-Faster Powder is useless!

We're never going to be ready on time!"
exclaimed the elf, throwing the bag of
powder down on the window ledge.

Ellie picked it up. "Something strange is
definitely going on," she said, peering into
the pouch at the Grow-Faster Powder
with a frown.

"Something is obviously really messing
up the magic in the Secret Kingdom,"
said Jasmine. "But what could it possibly
be?"

A loud cackle of laughter suddenly
echoed through the ballroom, filling the
air and making everyone jump. There
was a clap of thunder and the tall, bony
figure of Queen Malice appeared in the
centre of the floor.

"I might have the answer to that!"
she shrieked, holding up her black

thunderstaff. "I'm going to make *all* this silly Secret Kingdom magic stop working!" Her eyes gleamed like jet on either side of her pointy nose as she pointed her thunderstaff at Prince Felix. "First, I'm going to ruin your ball," she said and then she swung round and pointed her staff at King Merry. "And then I

shall take over the Secret Kingdom!"
"What do you mean, take over?"
demanded King Merry, putting his
hands on his hips. "How do you
think you can do that?"
Queen Malice laughed
in delight. "Just you
wait. Soon all the good
magic in the Secret

Kingdom will be gone forever. Look at
THIS!" She pulled a large hourglass from
under her black cloak with a flourish. It
had black sand running through it from
the top to the bottom, grain by grain.

King Merry's rosy cheeks turned pale.
"The Magic Hourglass! You've stolen it!"

"Yes, brother, dear. I stole it and I've
cursed the sand inside, which is why it is
now black instead of white," said Queen
Malice. "With every grain of sand that
trickles through it, a bit of good magic
drains out of the Secret Kingdom! When
all the sand has sprinkled through there
will be no good magic left. There will
just be MY magic! And I shall take
over and rule this land. Your pathetic
Golden Ball will become Queen Malice's
Black Ball, and no one shall be happy

apart from me – ME!"

With another shriek of laughter, she slammed her thunderstaff into the floor and disappeared in a cloud of nasty black smoke.

The Enchanted Objects

"Oh my goodness," breathed Jasmine as they all looked at each other in shock. "This is awful."

Summer nodded. "All the magic has been going wrong because of Queen Malice, just like we thought."

"We have to stop her," said Ellie. "We must get that hourglass back."

"You're quite right, dear – but how?" King Merry said, wringing his hands.

"The good magic in the kingdom is already not working properly, and we'll never be able to get the hourglass back without some really strong magic…"

"There has to be *something* we can do!" exclaimed Jasmine. Her mind was racing. "Let's think. There are lots of other magical objects in the Secret Kingdom – like King Merry's Spellbook, and the shield with the animal keepers on. Surely there must be something with enough magic to fight Queen Malice, even if she does have the hourglass."

King Merry scratched his head. "You know, you may be right! There *are* some magical objects that might be able to help. There are four special items in the kingdom that have extra-strong magical powers. They're called the Enchanted

Objects. They were made a long, long time ago, just in case anything like this ever happened. Whenever something magical is placed near one of the Enchanted Objects, the magical item's power will increase. If *all* the Enchanted Objects are collected together, their magic will be so strong that any curse can be defeated!"

"Great! Where are the objects?" Ellie asked eagerly.

"Ah." King Merry rubbed his nose. "That's the problem. To keep them safe, the four objects were scattered to the four corners of the kingdom – north, south, east and west – and no one was told exactly where they were."

"We'll find them," said Jasmine immediately. "There must be a way to work out where they are."

"There has to be," agreed Summer. The thought of the Secret Kingdom without good magic was awful.

King Merry spread his hands. "The trouble is, I don't even know what the four objects actually are."

"Wait a moment," said Prince Felix. "I'm sure I can remember my mother telling me about a very powerful fairy object called the Charmed Heart. She told me it's hidden somewhere in the forest around this palace."

"Do you think that might be one of the four Enchanted Objects?" said Ellie.

"It certainly could be," said King Merry. "Fairy magic is exceptionally strong."

"Can you remember anything more,

Prince Felix?" asked Trixi, flying around Felix's head and hovering in front of his nose. "Did your mother tell you where in the forest it was?"

"She said that it was hidden in a place called the Golden Grove but no one knows exactly where the Golden Grove is. It was always a bit of a myth amongst our kind. It's supposedly an enchanted place and the legend went that it would only be found when the kingdom had true need of it."

The prince shook his head. "I'm sorry. I wish I could be more helpful."

"I bet the Charmed Heart is one of the Enchanted Objects," said Jasmine. "I vote we leave right now and try to find the Golden Grove. The Secret Kingdom definitely needs its magic right now, so maybe we *will* be able to find it."

Ellie and Summer both nodded quickly.

"If the Golden Grove really is ready to be found, my ring might be able to take us there," said Trixi hopefully. She flew to King Merry. "Your Majesty, why don't you stay here with Prince Felix and get ready for the ball as best you can? The girls and I will try to find the Charmed Heart and get back as soon as possible."

King Merry nodded. "That sounds like a very good plan. Good luck, my dears!

Please hurry back!"

The girls held hands, and Trixi flew into the centre of their circle and tapped her ring. She called out:

"To the Golden Grove we need to go
To find the charm and defeat our foe!"

Nothing happened. Trixi tapped her ring again even harder.

"Perhaps it's not going to work," said Ellie, looking at her friends anxiously.

But just then, a faint spark of green light came from Trixi's ring, and the girls felt themselves being lifted into the air. They twirled slowly round and round, holding tightly onto each other's hands as the magic carried them out of the palace and through the woods. They spun

through the air, until the magic suddenly
dropped them and they landed with
a bump on a mossy bank. They rolled
to the bottom, and found themselves
surrounded by green trees and masses of
brambles.

"Are we at the grove?" said Jasmine,
blinking as she sat up.

"No," said Trixi. "The Golden Grove

must be a place of strong magic, but I can't feel any magic here at all — and the trees aren't golden."

"So where are we, then?" asked Summer.

"I don't know. I think we're somewhere in the middle of the woods. I'll try my ring again," Trixi said, looking at her pixie ring with a frown.

She tapped it and tapped it but nothing happened. She looked up anxiously. "This isn't good. All the magic in my ring seems to have faded. I'm not sure it will be able to take us anywhere now."

Ellie looked round at the trees and thick undergrowth. "What are we going to do?"

"Maybe the Golden Grove is somewhere near here," Summer said hopefully. "If we start walking we might find it."

"Good idea. It's better than just sitting round here anyway," said Jasmine.

They all set off. It was hard work pushing through the brambles. The thorns scratched their

bare legs and snagged their pretty beaded dresses, but none of the girls complained.

Soon they reached a path and it became easier to walk.

"Which way now, do you think?" said Jasmine when the path forked into two. "Left or right?"

There didn't seem anything to choose between the two paths. They both just led further into the trees.

"Maybe this way," said Ellie uncertainly, pointing to the left.

"No, wait!" said Trixi. She flew her leaf a little way down the right hand path and then down the left hand path. "Definitely the right!" she said, flying back. "When I fly that way my leaf goes faster. It feels like there's some strong magic coming from that direction that's pulling at it."

The girls exchanged excited looks. "It

could be pulling you towards the Golden Grove!" said Ellie.

They hurried along the right hand path. When that path also forked, they let Trixi's leaf guide them. It started getting quicker and quicker, zooming along in front of them so that Ellie, Summer and Jasmine had to run to keep up.

"Look at the trees," Summer exclaimed. "They're changing colour!"

They were. Gradually more and more bronze and gold trees were appearing amongst the green ones. The girls and Trixi took another turning, and soon the gold trees started to outnumber the bronze.

"We must be close!" panted Summer.

"That looks like a clearing ahead," said Jasmine, pointing to the far end of the path, where there was an arched entrance between the trees. "Maybe it's the Golden Grove!"

"Come on!" said Ellie eagerly – but just then, six grey shapes swooped down through the air and blocked the path. They had grey skin, hooked noses, beady eyes and grey, leathery wings like bats.

"Storm Sprites!" gasped Trixi, stopping

her leaf suddenly.

"Yes, it's us!" the Storm Sprites cackled. "Queen Malice sent us to stop you from finding the Charmed Heart!"

"But how did Queen Malice even know that's what we were doing?" said Jasmine in surprise.

"She's been spying on you with her crystal ball," said one of the sprites. "She's much cleverer than you silly girls. She heard you say you were going to find the Enchanted Objects and that you were starting with the Charmed Heart. Well, now we're here to stop you!"

"You can't stop us!" said Jasmine. "We're not scared of you!"

Ellie and Summer folded their arms and nodded sternly in agreement.

"But are you scared of ME?" Queen

Malice shrieked as she came swooping down on a small thundercloud, raising her staff…

✿Vicious Vines✿

Summer, Ellie, Jasmine and Trixi looked
up with shocked faces as Queen Malice
swept down towards them.

"Chase that pixie away from here!"
Queen Malice commanded her Storm
Sprites.

All six sprites flew at Trixi on their
leathery wings, with their bony fingers
outstretched. Trixi screamed and swerved
away on her leaf.

"Leave her alone!" shouted Jasmine,
throwing a golden pinecone from the
floor at the Storm Sprites.

They cackled
nastily as they
dodged it.
"Missed!"

"Get her!"
shrieked Queen
Malice.

One of the
sprites grabbed
at Trixi's
leaf and it
swerved
violently,
throwing
Trixi off.

"Help!"

she cried as she tumbled down into a
thick patch of vines at the side of the
path. Luckily, they cushioned her fall and
she bounced and sat up, unhurt.

Ellie and Summer ran over to check she
was all right while Jasmine threw more
pinecones at the Storm Sprites to keep
them away.

Summer crouched down. "Are you OK,
Trixi?"

"I'm fine, thanks," said Trixi.

Summer cupped her hands and
held them out for Trixi to climb into.
"Here, I'll carry you until we get your
leaf back."

BANG! A flash of lightning lit the air
as a thunderbolt shot from the end of
Queen Malice's black staff. It hit the
vines, and instantly, two of them reared

up and clamped like handcuffs around
Summer's wrists.

"What's happening?" Summer said in
alarm.

Suddenly more vines began to snake
towards the girls, and
Ellie squealed as
their tendrils
wound around
her ankles. She
tried to kick
out, but they
held her fast,
and when
she tried to
pull them
off with her
fingers, more
vines moved

around
her
wrists,
tightening
quickly.
"The vines are
attacking us!" she
shouted.

Jasmine ran over.

"No, stay back, Jasmine!"
Summer cried – but it was too
late. Jasmine yelled as the vines
caught her too. Now they were
all trapped! Even Trixi had tendrils
tightening around her tiny ankles. They
struggled and struggled, but the vines
held them fast. Queen Malice swooped
towards them on her thundercloud,
grinning nastily.

"Let us go, Queen Malice!" shouted Jasmine angrily.

The Queen laughed. "No! You'll be stuck here while my Storm Sprites and I go to the Golden Grove to find that silly Charmed Heart. You'll never stop my plans. Never!" She rose from the ground on her thundercloud and shot off along the path towards the grove.

"Bye, bye, cabbage brains!" shrieked the Storm Sprites, flying after Queen Malice. The girls and Trixi watched them go in dismay.

"We've got to get free!" said Jasmine in frustration. She pulled and kicked at the vines but the thick, furry stems were wrapped firmly around her wrists and ankles and she couldn't break their grip.

Trixi tapped her ring, but nothing

happened. "It's no use. I can't use magic to free us. My ring's still not working."

"If we can't escape with magic then we'll have to find another way," said Summer. "Can anyone see any sharp rocks or stones that we could use to cut through the vines?"

They all looked around, but there were just the horrible vines and nothing else.

As Ellie squirmed, she felt a lump in the pocket of her dress. What was it? She reached into her pocket and found a small bag of silver powder.

"What's that?" said Summer.

"It's the Grow-Faster Powder the elves were using at the Golden Palace. I was looking at it when Queen Malice appeared," Ellie said. "I must have put it in my pocket without thinking."

Jasmine looked alarmed. "Well, don't spill it, we don't want the vines to grow any more!"

Ellie was about to put it back into her pocket when Summer gasped. "Wait! Remember the powder wasn't working properly? It was making the flowers at the palace *shrink* not grow. Maybe if we put some on these vines they'll shrink too!"

"But what if the powder *does* work properly?" said Jasmine doubtfully.

"We'll be even more stuck," said Ellie.

"If we don't try, we'll be stuck here forever anyway," said Summer. She turned to Trixi. "What do you think?"

Trixi's eyebrows knitted in concern, but she nodded. "I think we should try it and see what happens," she said. "It's the only hope we've got."

"OK, then." Ellie took a pinch of the powder out of the bag and looked at the others. "Here goes!"

She sprinkled the glittering powder on the vines that were wrapped around her hands and ankles. They all held their breath. What was the powder going to do?

Pitfall!

Please work, please work, Ellie thought as the Grow-Faster Powder sparkled on the furry green vines.

All of a sudden, the vines began to go brown and shrivel up. They released their grip on Ellie. "I'm free!" she said in delight.

She jumped to her feet and quickly scattered powder over the vines that were binding the others.

"Hooray!" Jasmine said, standing up quickly as the vines all shrank to dry brown strands.

Trixi whistled loudly, and her leaf rose up from where it was resting on the forest floor and came flying over to her. She leapt onto it. "Right! Let's get to the Golden Grove as fast as we can!"

"Come on!" said Jasmine, setting off at a run.

The others raced after her. They could see the Golden Grove at the end of the path. They jumped over tree roots, their feet kicking up fallen leaves as they ran. Had Queen Malice already found the Charmed Heart?

Please don't let us be too late, thought Jasmine as they got closer to the entrance. She glanced over her shoulder. "Quick, we have to— WOAH!" She broke off with a shriek as the ground suddenly vanished beneath her feet.

She heard the others yell as they all fell downwards. Jasmine's arms windmilled as she braced herself for a crashing fall.

THUMP!

She landed in the middle of an enormous mound of soft feathers. THUMP! THUMP! She heard Summer and Ellie land beside her. They all sank deep into the feather pile and had to struggle back up to the surface. They poked their heads out.

"What just happened?" Summer said in shock.

Ellie saw a round opening above them. Through it she could see the sky. "I think we've fallen into a big pit."

"You have!" Trixi flew down towards them on her leaf. "It was covered by lots of leaves. As you ran over it the leaves gave way. Are you all OK?"

Ellie, Summer and Jasmine all nodded. The feathers had cushioned their fall perfectly. They were lovely and soft.

"It's... It's sort of *pretty* in here," said Summer, realising there were strands of little glittering stars hanging around the pit walls, giving off a dim, twinkling light.

"Do you think Queen Malice conjured up the pit to stop us?" said Ellie.

Summer shook her head. "Queen Malice would have put thorns and brambles at the bottom, not feathers and shining stars."

As she spoke, a cute little brown rabbit poked its head out of a hole in the side of the pit. It blinked at them curiously.

"Summer's right. Queen Malice would never have set a trap like this," agreed Jasmine.

"So who *did* set it, then?" said Ellie, puzzled.

Jasmine had an idea. "Do you remember the Ancient Egyptians and how they used to put traps in the tunnels

that led into the centre of the pyramids?"
Summer and Ellie nodded. "Well, maybe
this trap was put here by whoever hid the
Charmed Heart, to stop people getting to
the Golden Grove. It's a nice trap made
by people who use good magic."

"If you're right, it must mean we're
very close to the Charmed Heart," said
Trixi.

"We might be close, but we're still
trapped," Summer said.

"What I don't understand is why
Queen Malice didn't fall into this trap,"
said Ellie.

"She was flying, like me," said Trixi.
"Remember, she was on her thunder
cloud, and her Storm Sprites were flying
along with her. The trap would only
work if someone ran across the leaves."

"Of course," said Summer. "Oh, I wish we could fly out of here!"

Trixi looked at her ring and gasped. "Maybe you can!" She held her ring out. "Look!" The ring was glowing green, the centre glittering brightly. "My ring's magic is much stronger now. The Enchanted Objects are so full of magical power they make all magical things around them stronger. The Charmed Heart must be affecting my ring! I can try to use it to get you out of here." Trixi tapped her ring and called out a spell:

"All three friends be feather-light
Float up high to where it's bright."

The three girls exclaimed as they felt all the weight vanish from their bodies

and they started to rise up into the air
towards the circle of sunlight.

"We're floating!" cried Ellie.

Jasmine laughed in delight and twirled
round. "It's like swimming in the air!"

Summer kicked with her legs and
whooshed upwards even faster. "This is so
much fun!"

Trixi giggled as she flew up beside them
on her leaf.

Ellie turned a somersault. "I feel like
I'm an astronaut in space!"

The girls held hands and all kicked
hard with their feet. They zoomed
upwards and flew out of the hole. Trixi
tapped her ring again and the magic
gently brought them down. As their feet
touched the ground, they felt heaviness
flood back into their bodies.

"That was amazing!" said Ellie. "Thanks, Trixi!"

"I'm just pleased my ring is working again," said Trixi.

"Let's get to the Golden Grove – but be careful, everyone," said Jasmine. "Keep your eyes out for more traps!"

The girls cautiously approached the entrance to the grove.

"What's that noise?" said Ellie, hearing some strange muffled shouts.

They swapped puzzled looks.

"It seems to be coming from above us," said Jasmine. She glanced up. "Oh my goodness!" she gasped. "Look!"

The Charmed Heart!

High up in the trees that arched over the entrance, Queen Malice and her Storm Sprites were all caught in giant white cocoons made from fluffy spider webs.

"What are they doing?" said Summer.

"It must be a trap for people flying into the grove!" said Trixi. "Maybe they didn't see the webs until it was too late!"

The cocoons wriggled and swayed as the queen and the storm sprites struggled to break free.

Queen Malice spotted the girls. "Help me! Get me out of this ridiculous web!" she shouted.

"Let me see." Jasmine pretended to consider it. "Umm…no!"

Summer, Ellie and Trixi giggled as the queen screeched in fury.

"Come on," said Ellie. "Let's go into the grove and find the Charmed Heart!"

"No!" shrieked Queen Malice.

They ignored her and went cautiously through the entrance. As the girls stepped into the circular clearing, their breath caught in awe. Every blade of grass was golden, and there were clumps of tiny golden daisies scattered through the grass.

The air was filled with golden butterflies
and the smell of sweetest honeysuckle.

"This place is really magical,"
whispered Trixi. "Look at how brightly
my ring is glowing." Her ring was now
shining like a mini-lantern on her finger.

"I wonder where the Charmed Heart is," said Jasmine in a low voice. Somehow it felt wrong to speak loudly in such a peaceful place.

"I think my leaf might be able to find it," said Trixi. "Do you remember how I felt like it was being pulled towards the clearing? Well, I can feel it wanting to move right now." The girls could see her leaf was visibly trembling, as if it was taking an enormous effort for it just to stay in the place where Trixi wanted it to be. "Should I see where it leads if I let it just go where it wants?" said Trixi.

The others nodded eagerly, and Trixi stroked her leaf's green surface.

"Lovely leaf, fly where you will
Find us the heart, then please be still."

She sat back and the leaf flew across the clearing, as if it was being pulled by an invisible thread. It flew to the very centre of the clearing and then stopped and hovered for a moment before sinking to the ground and landing on a patch of daisies. Summer, Ellie and Jasmine all ran over and knelt down beside Trixi and her leaf.

"Here?" said Trixi, in surprise. "But these are just daisies. I can't see any sign of the Charmed Heart."

"Unless it's buried in the soil underneath the daisies?" said Jasmine hopefully. She started digging in the soft soil with her bare hands, frowning in concentration.

"We'd better hurry," said Ellie, hearing the shouts from outside the clearing getting louder. "It sounds like Queen Malice is starting to break free."

"I've found something!" Jasmine gasped. She pulled out a wooden chest. It had a heart carved into the lid and a golden clasp.

"Open it!" Summer urged her in excitement.

Jasmine opened the clasp and the lid sprang open. Golden light flooded out, and inside the chest, nestled on a bed of pink silk, was a large, glowing crystal heart.

"The Charmed Heart!" Trixi said in

an awed voice.

"We'd better take it to King Merry straight away," said Summer.

"Can you use your ring to transport us, Trixi?" said Ellie.

Trixi nodded. "While it's near the heart it will work perfectly."

They all stood up, with Jasmine carefully holding the box, but then suddenly there came a shout.

"Stop right there!"

Queen Malice came charging into the clearing. She was holding her skirts up above her bony knees with one hand and had cobwebs hanging from her hair. "You're not going to get away with this!" She raised her thunderstaff and pointed it at them.

"That Charmed Heart will be mine!"

Back to the Palace

"Quick, Trixi!" Jasmine yelled.

Trixi was already shouting a spell.

*"Pixie ring, whisk us away
To the Golden Palace, no delay!"*

A black lightning bolt exploded from the end of the queen's staff and shot across the clearing towards them. At the same moment, the girls grabbed hands and, just in time, they were transported away in a flash of bright green light.

They landed almost instantly, back in the grounds of the Golden Palace.

"Oh, thank goodness," said Ellie, taking a breath. "We're safe!"

Summer's heart was pounding in her chest. "Phew! That was close!"

"And we have the Charmed Heart!" said Jasmine, holding out the box.

"But things aren't looking so good here," said Trixi glancing round at the gardens. There was grey sagging paper bunting on the trees, and lots of wilted rose bushes. "The palace really doesn't look ready for a ball, and it must be almost time for the guests to arrive."

"My friends, my dear friends!" They heard King Merry's voice and swung round. The king was at the top of the steps that led from the ballroom into the garden. His top hat was falling off his head and his glasses were slipping down his nose. "Oh, I'm very glad you're back safely."

"We found the Charmed Heart, Your Majesty," said Jasmine, running up the steps with the chest the crystal heart was nestled inside.

"You did? Oh, thank you so much!" said King Merry as Jasmine handed it to him. "I knew I could depend on you all. As soon as the ball is over, I shall take it back to my palace for safe-keeping."

"How have things been going here, Your Majesty?" Trixi asked, looking around again anxiously. "It seems like the palace still isn't ready for the ball…"

"It's awful, Trixi," King Merry said. "Poor Prince Felix is very upset. The guests are due to arrive any minute, but with the magic draining away everything's carried on going wrong. There's no food, no fruit punch, no decorations, no music…"

"Trixi's ring can help with that," said
Ellie. "It's working again now that it's
been close to the Charmed Heart!"

"Oh yes! Of course! And the Charmed
Heart *itself* should be able to start
making things right too," said King
Merry. "Now let me see – what will
happen if…?"

He opened the chest. The Charmed
Heart was shining like a star inside it.
There was a bright
golden flash and
suddenly the
Charmed Heart
floated up into
the air, over
King Merry's
head and into the

ballroom. It carried on floating higher
and higher until it reached the ceiling.
Then it hovered in one spot
and started to slowly
spin round like a disco
ball. Glittering light
shone off it, and before
the girls' delighted eyes,
things started to change. The
stale bread on the table transformed into
delicious looking party food. The empty
crystal jugs filled up with pretty pink
fruit punch, the No Hand Band started
to play a jaunty tune, and the floating
dance floor rose up into the air.

Ellie glanced behind her into the
garden. "Look!"

The magic was working there too.
Flowers were blooming and brightening;

the grey scraps of paper bunting had
turned into twinkling golden stars, and
pretty lanterns appeared along the edges
of the paths, each one glowing with a
different colour of the rainbow.

Trixi flew over the girls' heads and
tapped her ring. Their dirty, torn dresses
instantly turned beautiful again, their

hair was sleek and brushed, and their tiaras glittered. "Come on!" she cried as they gasped in delight. "The guests will be here any second."

Trixi flew into the ballroom, and Summer, Ellie and Jasmine ran after her with King Merry, just as the doors at the other end flew open.

Prince Felix was standing there. "This is fantastic!" he cried in delight. "I don't know what's happened, but everything seems to be sorting itself out!" He noticed the girls and Trixi. "Oh, you're back! Is this all your doing?"

The girls raced over and told him what had been happening. They had just finished when a large gong rang out from the hall. King Merry jumped up and down in excitement, his tummy jiggling. "Ooh, Prince Felix! Your guests are here!"

Prince Felix beamed. "Then let's go and welcome them all inside!"

It was the most wonderful ball the girls had ever been to. The elf butlers served the glittery fruit punch in golden goblets and soon everyone was laughing and dancing, taking breaks to eat the delicious food – finger sandwiches with fillings that could turn into whatever type you wished for, bowls of dewberries and the sweetest cherries, and tiny star-shaped biscuits that exploded into sugar crystals when you put one in your mouth.

Even Ellie, with her fear of heights, had to admit how much fun it was when the girls were swept up onto the floating dance floor. They swirled around together to a wonderful waltz. Then they all held hands with King Merry and Trixi, and danced around in a circle while the Charmed Heart sparkled and glittered overhead.

King Merry jigged about, his plump cheeks pink with all the excitement, his glasses crooked on his nose. "Castles and coronations! Isn't this splendid?" he kept saying.

"It's amazing!" said Jasmine. She'd never been on a floating dance floor before. It was so amazing to be hovering up high in the air!

Eventually they were all so exhausted they slid down the slide that led to the ground, and found four golden chairs at the side of the room. Trixi hovered beside them on her leaf.

"I'm so glad that the magic has returned to the Golden Palace," King Merry said, looking round at everyone enjoying the ball. "If it hadn't been for you all finding the Charmed Heart, this ball would have been a disaster."

"We're going to have to find the other three Enchanted Objects as soon as possible," Jasmine said.

"Before Queen Malice finds them," Ellie added.

Summer nodded. "And before the rest of the kingdom's magic drains away."

"King Merry and I will do our best to find out where the three remaining Enchanted Objects are hidden," said Trixi. "As soon as we know, we'll send you a message."

"We'll do everything we can to stop

Queen Malice," Jasmine said.

"Thank you," said King Merry. "For
now, my friends, I think it is time to say
goodbye – but we will see you again
very soon!"

Summer, Ellie and Jasmine nodded and
held hands. Trixi flew round and kissed
them all on their noses and then tapped
her ring. A cloud of sparkles swirled out
and the girls found themselves being spun
away.

They landed back at school, hidden
behind the Reception classroom with the
Magic Box between them. As usual, no
time had passed since they had left for
the Secret Kingdom.

"We're back," said Summer. "Doesn't
it feel strange? It was all so bright and
sparkly at the ball and here, well, it's just

not quite as exciting."

"And we've got our school uniform on
again," said Jasmine with a sigh.

"It's probably good that we have," said
Ellie with a smile. "Can you imagine
everyone's faces if we turned up after
break in our party dresses?"

They all giggled.

"So much has just happened," said
Jasmine, putting the Magic Box back
in Ellie's bag. "It feels like we should be
going to bed, not doing more school
work!"

"We'd better keep checking the Magic
Box," said Ellie. "There's no knowing
when King Merry will send us a
message."

"I hope it's soon," said Summer. "I hate
the thought of Queen Malice trying to

drain all the magic away from the Secret Kingdom."

"Me too. We have to stop her," said Jasmine.

Ellie nodded. "The Secret Kingdom needs us."

Summer took her friends' hands. "And whenever the Secret Kingdom needs us, we'll always be there, won't we?"

"Always!" Jasmine and Ellie declared, as they all grinned at one another. They'd be sure to have another magical adventure very soon!

**In the next Secret Kingdom
adventure, Ellie, Summer and
Jasmine experience**

Mermaid Magic

Read on for a sneak peek...

A Message
from Trixi

"Can I have the butterfly cutter first,
please?" asked Summer Hammond.

She was in her kitchen with her
best friends, Jasmine Smith and Ellie
MacDonald. They all wore aprons
over their pretty summer dresses,
because they were making biscuits
for their school bake sale to raise money

for new library books.

Jasmine handed it to her. "I'm making star biscuits," she said. "I'm going to sprinkle them with edible glitter when they're cooked so they twinkle like real stars."

Ellie grinned. "That's a great idea! I'm going to use the mermaid cutter and decorate the tails with chocolate buttons."

Summer's two little brothers, Finn and Connor, dashed into the kitchen. "Aren't your biscuits ready yet?" Connor asked, disappointed. "We want to try them."

"You can have a couple of chocolate buttons," Summer said, handing her brothers a few.

"Thanks!" the boys exclaimed. They ran out again, munching happily.

Summer rolled her dough and began

cutting out butterfly shapes. She pushed the kitchen door shut with her foot, then said in a low voice, "It's too bad my butterfly biscuits can't fly, like the Catch-Me Cookies we ate in Candy Cove. They'd be the hit of the bake sale!"

The girls exchanged excited looks. Candy Cove was in the Secret Kingdom, a magical land ruled by jolly King Merry. It was full of elves, giants, pixies and other amazing creatures — and the girls loved to visit.

"I wonder when Trixi will come for us," Jasmine said. When they were needed in the Secret Kingdom, their pixie friend, Trixi, always sent them a message through a magic box that they shared.

"Soon, I hope," said Ellie. "I can't wait to see her and King Merry again."

The girls finished cutting out their biscuits and arranged them on baking sheets. Ellie popped them in the oven and Jasmine set the timer. As it began to tick, she sighed loudly.

"What's wrong?" asked Summer.

"The timer's just reminded me about Queen Malice's hourglass," Jasmine replied.

King Merry's mean sister, Queen Malice, had put a curse on the Secret Kingdom and as black sand trickled through her magical hourglass it was gradually destroying all the good magic there. It was causing problems across the land, and once all the sand had run through there'd be no good magic left in the kingdom at all.

Ellie shivered. "Remember how horrible

it was in the Secret Kingdom when Queen Malice took over before?"

"We stopped her then, and we'll stop her again," said Jasmine determinedly. "We've already found the Charmed Heart. Once we find the other three Enchanted Objects, her curse will be lifted."

King Merry's ancestors had carefully hidden four Enchanted Objects in distant corners of the Secret Kingdom. The girls were trying to find them all because their powerful magic would destroy Queen Malice's curse, but they'd been so well hidden, so long ago, that even King Merry didn't know where they were. To make things worse, Queen Malice was searching for the objects, too!

"Let's check the Magic Box," suggested

Summer. "Maybe Trixi's sent us a message."

"Good idea!" agreed Ellie and Jasmine.

The girls raced upstairs to Summer's bedroom. It was a cosy room with walls decorated with animal posters and shelves crammed with books. Ellie closed the door so Summer's brothers wouldn't see what they were doing, while Summer pulled the Magic Box out from underneath her bed. It was a beautiful box, carved with mermaids, unicorns and other magical creatures. A mirror, surrounded by six glittering gems, was set into the top.

"The mirror's glowing!" Summer cried eagerly. She hurriedly set the box on the bed and they all crowded round.

"Here comes Trixi's riddle," said Jasmine

as words began to appear in the mirror.
She read it out:

"This place of learning lies beneath
The shimmering turquoise sea.
Here long-haired swimmers
Study hard to learn their A B C."

Read
Mermaid Magic
to find out what
happens next!

Have you read all the books in Series Seven?

When the last grain of sand falls in Queen Malice's cursed hourglass, magic will be lost from the Secret Kingdom forever!
Can Ellie, Summer and Jasmine find all the Enchanted Objects and break the spell?

Look out for the latest special!

Out now!

Queen Malice's spell on the Magic Hourglass is making everything in the Secret Kingdom go wonky! Can you help the girls put things right by spotting the five differences in the pictures below?

Competition!

Those naughty Storm Sprites are up to no good again. They have trampled through this book and left muddy footprints on one of the pages!

Did you spot them while you were reading this book?

Can you find the pages where the cheeky sprites have left their footprints in each of the four books in series 7?
When you have found all four sets of footprints, go online and tell us which pages they are on to enter the competition at

www.secretkingdombooks.com

We will put all of the correct entries into a draw and select a winner to receive a special Secret Kingdom goody bag!

Alternatively send entries to:
Secret Kingdom, Series 7 Competition
Orchard Books, Carmelite House, 50 Victoria Embankment,
London, EC4Y 0DZ

Don't forget to add your name and address.

Good luck!

Closing date: 29th February 2016

Secret Kingdom

A magical world of
friendship and fun!

Join the Secret Kingdom Club at

www.secretkingdombooks.com

and enjoy games, sneak peeks and lots more!

You'll find great activities, competitions, stories
and games, plus a special newsletter for
Secret Kingdom friends!